Watching...

translation
Sarah Adams

story
Suzy Chic

illustrations
Monique Touvay

D1406777

WingedChariot Press

Every morning
I went to see...

Every morning
I went to see
a little tree
I'd taken a shine to.

One day
it held out a flower
from one
of its branches...

And said:
"This is for you."

"But if you don't
pick it straight away,
if you wait,
the flower will change
into a fruit."

I asked the tree
to keep the flower
for me
for a day,
so I could think
about it...

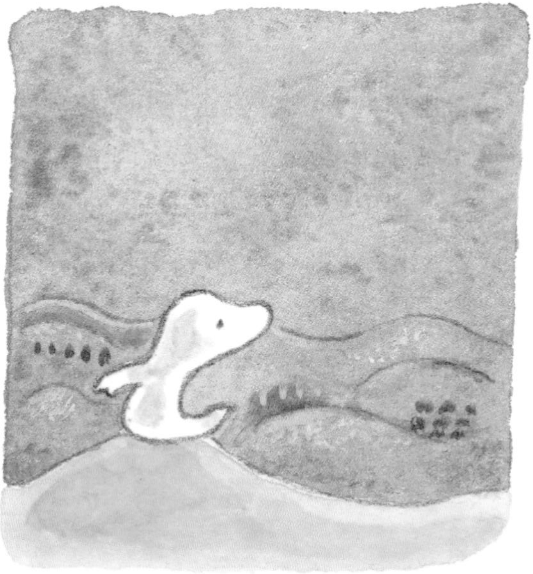

I thought about it
and went back
the next day,
at ten o'clock,
and the next day too.

And every day
after that,
at the same time.

I wanted
to find out
what kind of fruit
could possibly come
from a flower
like that.

The flower
turned into
a shiny
green fruit.

The little tree
said to me:
" You can pick it,
it's yours,
but if you wait
a day or two,
the fruit will ripen,
and you'll be able
to eat it. "

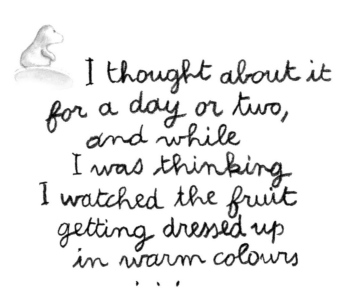

I thought about it
for a day or two,
and while
I was thinking
I watched the fruit
getting dressed up
in warm colours
. . .

One morning,
the tree said :

"It's nice
and ripe now;
you can pick it.

But if you bury it,
it'll sprout
and a new tree
will grow."

So I stopped
thinking,
and agreed.

Some ants
helped me organise
a special ceremony
to bury
the fruit.

But it still worried me seeing that promise of hope disappearing.

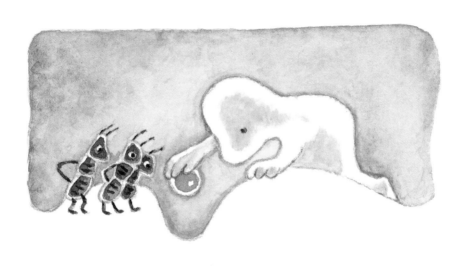

I waited
and watched
and watched

and waited ...

Then
one day,
a seedling
appeared.

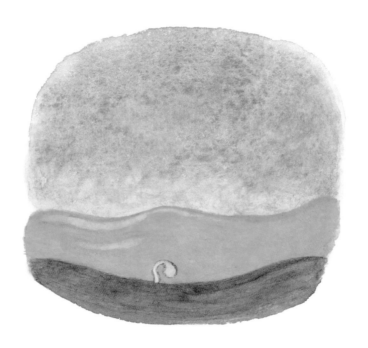

One morning
I went
to water
it,

and
from the tip
of
its first leaf,
the tiny tree
whispered:

thank you...